SHOULD You Have Fries with That?

Dear Reader

One of the most popular fast foods in the world is fries or chips. We're often asked by fast food restaurants, "Do you want fries with that?"

In this book, we're going to prepare you for a debate in Chapter 5 called, "Should you have fries with that?"

> "MAKE SURE AN ADULT IS ALWAYS WITH YOU WHEN COOKING FRIES!"

Before you debate this topic, research the information in the first four chapters.

I hope you enjoy reading about potatoes and fries as much as I enjoyed writing about them ... and eating them, too!

Sharon Parsons

For learning solutions, visit cengage.com.au

Contents

1 Potatoes or Fries?

Are **Potatoes** Healthy?

Yes, potatoes help keep us healthy. They contain energy in the form of carbohydrates. If a potato is eaten with the skin on, it will be high in vitamin C, too. Potatoes also contain fibre, minerals and other vitamins, which our bodies need to stay healthy.

Why Are Fries Thin?

Fries are long, thin strips of potato. They are thin so they can cook quickly in oil or fat.

WHAT'S VITAMIN C?

Vitamin C is essential to the human body. Eating foods with vitamin C helps the immune system fight off viruses and also assists the body to heal any injuries it may have.

History

A History of French Fries

In the 1800s, France was one of the first countries to deep fry potato strips. "French" relates to the way the fries are cut into very thin strips, like matchsticks.

What Do YOU Call Fries?

Potatoes can become **LESS** healthy when we:

- deep fry them in oil
- peel the skin off
- make potato chips.

Potatoes are **MORE** healthy when we:

- bake them in the oven with the skin on
- boil or steam them
- mash them with milk and a little olive oil or butter.

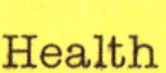

Health

How Many Vegetables Each Day?

Nutritionists say we should eat between three and five serves of vegetables every day. Try to eat vegetables of different colours, such as:

- red (tomatoes)
- orange (carrots)
- green (broccoli)
- brown/white (potatoes)
- yellow (squash)

Trans Fat Oils

Restaurants and fast food shops may cook fries in oils that contain trans fats.

Small amounts of trans fats can be found in meat and dairy products. Food with trans fats lasts longer than other foods. But trans fats are unhealthy.

Scientists warn that trans fats may cause cancer and heart disease.

Not Hot Enough

If the oil for frying is not hot enough, fries can soak up extra oil.

Eating too much oil and fat can make people less healthy and overweight.

There are a good range of vegetable oils to choose from.

Oils or Butter?

Most vegetable oils are healthy if they are not processed too much. Cooking oils made from vegetables are healthier than cooking oils made from animal products, such as butter. Good cooking oils include canola oil, sunflower oil and safflower oil.

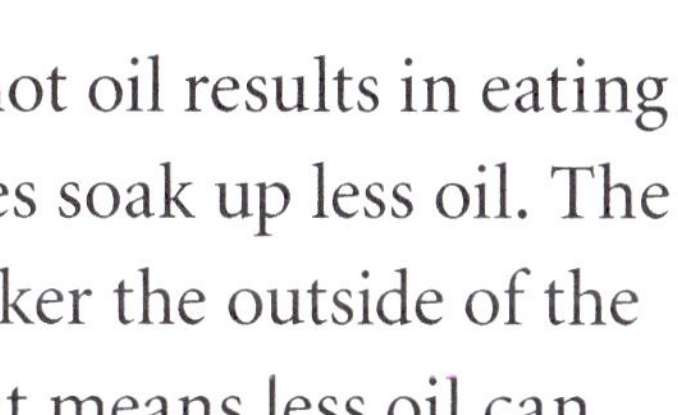

Frying Fries in HOT Oil

Frying fries in a very hot oil results in eating less fat because the fries soak up less oil. The hotter the oil, the quicker the outside of the fries crisp up, too. That means less oil can get into the inside of the potato.

BAKE Fries in the Oven

Baking fries in the oven in a little oil is a healthier way to cook them. Also, baking fries destroys fewer vitamins in the potatoes as they cook.

2 A Healthy Potato Pyramid

EAT LESS

Fries made from peeled potatoes and cooked in animal-based oil

Fries made from peeled potatoes and cooked in hot vegetable oil

Fries made from unpeeled potatoes and cooked in hot vegetable oil

Peeled, oven-baked potatoes

Oven-baked or boiled potatoes with the skin left on

EAT MORE

Who Invented Potato Chips?

A chef called George Crum from the USA invented the snack we know as potato chips or crisps, in 1853. One night, he cooked French fries for a guest at a restaurant. But the guest sent the French fries back to George because they were too thick.

a painting of George Crum

George sliced a potato into very thin slices and cooked them in extra hot oil. They turned out thin and crispy, and the guest loved them! George became famous for his potato chips.

Chips are a crunchy snack!

3 Compare Two Recipes for Fries

A **Shallow-Fried** Fries Recipe

The two recipes in this chapter will help you with your research for the debate in Chapter 5.

Step 1

Scrub all dirt off the potatoes. Keep the skin on for the vitamin C.

It's healthier!

Step 2

Ask an adult to help you.

Cut each potato in half. Cut each half into slices, and then slice each piece into strips to form fries.

Step 3

Pour in enough oil to just cover the base of the frying pan.

Better for your health!

Fries can be cooked in an oven, too.

Step 4

Put the pan on the stove. Turn on the stove and heat the oil. To check that the oil is hot enough, carefully drop a potato strip into the pan. If it sizzles, the oil is hot enough.

Step 5

Put the potato strips into the frying pan. Be extra careful not to splash the hot oil.

Step 6

Cook one side of the fries for about five minutes until they look golden.

Step 7

Remove the frying pan from the stove.

Step 8

Turn the fries over with a fork or an egg flip.

Step 9

Put the frying pan back onto the stove. Cook the other side of the fries until golden.

Step 10

Turn off the stove.

Remove the frying pan from the stove.

Step 11

Drain the fries in a sieve or on a plate with some absorbent paper.

Better for your health!

Step 12

When drained, put the fries on a serving plate. If you want salt, sprinkle with a little **iodised sea salt**.

IODISED SALT

Everyone needs iodine in tiny amounts to stay healthy. Iodised salt has enough iodine added to it to keep people healthy.

Step 13

When the fries have cooled a little, eat and enjoy!

A **Deep-Fried** Fries Recipe

Make sure an adult is ALWAYS with you while you're cooking.

Step 1

Wash and peel potatoes. Cut each potato in half. Cut each half into slices, and then slice each piece into strips to form fries.

Peel the potatoes.

COMPOSTING

If you have a compost bin, put the potato peels into it. Compost is good for the garden.

Step 2

Fill the deep fryer with oil. Turn it on to heat, so the oil becomes very hot.

Step 3

Put the potato strips into the deep-fryer's basket. **Then put the basket into the deep-fryer.**

deep frying fries

Step 4

Cook the fries for about 10–12 minutes until golden and crisp.

Turn off the deep fryer.

Carefully lift up the deep-fryer's basket.

Gently shake the basket. Allow the oil to drain from the fries.

Put the fries on a plate with some absorbent paper. If you want salt, sprinkle the fries with a little **iodised salt**.

Better for your health!

When the fries are cool enough, eat and enjoy!

Which of the two recipes is the healthiest way to cook fries?

a) the shallow-fried fries
b) the deep-fried fries

4 Do You Want Sauce with That?

What Do **You** Like on **Fries?**

Most people like to sprinkle something onto their fries. Some like salt; others like sauce; some like vinegar; and some like mayonnaise. Some people love them all!

Health

Sea Salt

Regular salt is mined from the ground. Sea salt comes from seawater. Scientists say that sea salt is healthier than table salt as it has more minerals in it.

sea salt crystals

Fry Sauce

Tomato sauce is a favourite sauce for fries.

In parts of the USA, fry sauce is served with fries. It can be made by mixing two-thirds tomato sauce and one-third mayonnaise.

Fry sauce = 2/3 tomato sauce and 1/3 mayonnaise

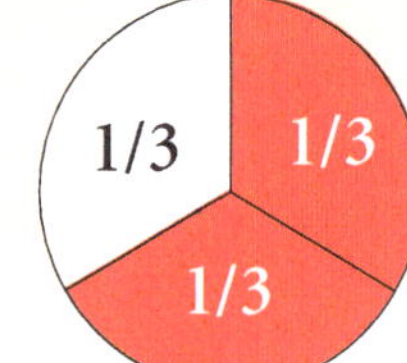

Hidden Salt

Everybody needs to have some salt in their diets. But too much salt is not good for us. Many processed foods have lots of added salt, so we may unknowingly eat far more salt than we need. Find out the salt content of packaged foods on their labels.

Eating too much salt is unhealthy.

vinegar in a bottle

Vinegar

In many parts of the world, people love to sprinkle vinegar on their fries or dip them in vinegar.

Some of the most popular vinegars are malt vinegar, cider vinegar and balsamic vinegar.

5 A Debate: Should You Have Fries with That?

What Is a **Debate?**

A debate is a discussion between two teams, where each team represents a different side of an argument. In this book, the debate is between two imaginary teams. Each team presents opposite sides of the argument for the debate, "Should you have fries with that?"

Debate Teams

On pages 18 and 19, one team argues for the debate topic and the other team argues against it. The team with the most points wins the debate.

Debate Judge

Every debate has a judge or an adjudicator. Our debate walrus character is the judge for this debate. The walrus will score each team on page 20.

getting ready to debate

Our Debate Walrus Says:

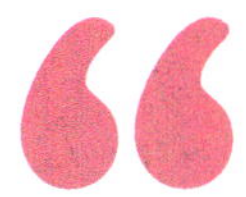

We all know that fries are one of the most popular fast foods. Some fast food places ask people, "Do you want fries with that?"

Our debate topic is: "Should you have fries with that?"

One team will argue "for" fries and the other team will argue "against" fries. After hearing each team present their arguments "for" and "against" the topic, I will decide which team wins the debate.

Debate Topic:
Should You Have Fries with That?

mmmm!

"For" Eating Fries

"FOR" Team LEADER
"We are here to argue that we should eat fries. Our research tells us that there are many reasons why we should eat fries."

"FOR" Team Member 2
"First, we all know that fries are made from potatoes. They are a vegetable and that means they are healthy for us."

"Against" Eating Fries

"AGAINST" Team LEADER
"Today, our team will argue that fries, especially fries from fast food places, should not be eaten."

"AGAINST" Team Member 2
"Potatoes are healthy but the topic is about fries. Fast food fries are not healthy as they're cooked in unhealthy oil."

Mmm, I love fries!

Fries for a treat!

Hmm, are fries healthy or not?

To fry or not to fry?

I Love Fries!

Good oil vs. bad oil

"FOR" Team Member 3

"Potatoes are high in many vitamins, like vitamin C, to keep us healthy. Potatoes contain carbohydrates. We need carbohydrate foods for energy. At school, we play a lot of sports to keep fit, so we need potatoes to give us energy."

"FOR" Team Member 4

"Cooking fries in oil is okay if it's a good oil. We know that fries cooked in hot vegetable oil and then well drained afterwards are healthy."

"FOR" Team LEADER

"To summarise, we answer **YES** to the question, 'Should you have fries with that?' Fries are potatoes, and potatoes are an important food that gives us energy and keeps us healthy."

"AGAINST" Team Member 3

"Potatoes are healthy for us but remember the topic is about fries! Most fast food fries are cooked without their skin so the vitamin C is removed."

"AGAINST" Team Member 4

"Yes, cooking fries in vegetable oil is better for our health. But in our research we found out that most fast food fries are cooked in trans fat oils. Nutritionists tell us that trans fats cause many health problems."

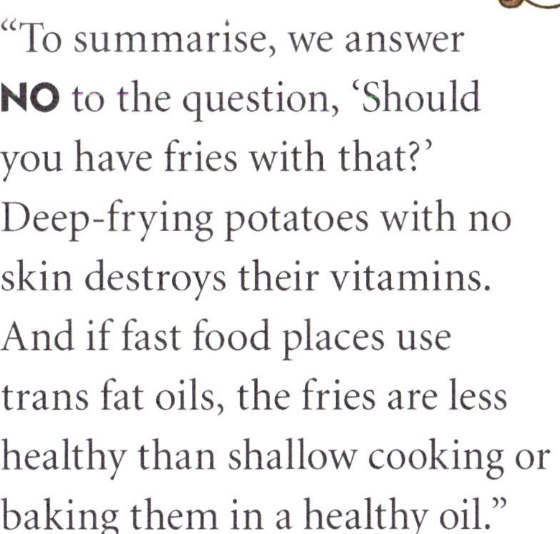

"AGAINST" Team LEADER

"To summarise, we answer **NO** to the question, 'Should you have fries with that?' Deep-frying potatoes with no skin destroys their vitamins. And if fast food places use trans fat oils, the fries are less healthy than shallow cooking or baking them in a healthy oil."

See page 20 for the winning team!

Our **Debate** Walrus **Decides**

Both teams have presented their arguments. But I have added up the points for each team and the winning team has won by **one** point!

The Winning Team

The winner of the debate is the team that answered **NO** to the question. The main reason is that:

- many fast food places do use trans fat oils to cook fries
- vitamin C is lost when the skin is peeled off and most fast food fries are cooked without skin.

Look at the Healthy Potato Pyramid on page 8 to see the healthiest way to cook potatoes. The pyramid also shows that we can eat fast food fries as a treat from time to time!

6 A Fast Food Game

How to Play **Straws** and **Stems**

You can play Straws and Stems exactly like Snakes and Ladders. Throw the dice and when you land on an unhealthy fact, slide down a drinking straw. When you land on a healthy fact, climb up a potato plant's stem.

History

The History of Snakes and Ladders

Hundreds of years ago, the game of Snakes and Ladders began in India. By the late 1890s, it was being played in England. In 1943 it became Chutes and Ladders in the USA.

children playing Snakes and Ladders

TURN THE PAGE TO PLAY!

Straws and Stems **GAME**

FINISH
You ate 12 deep-fried chicken nuggets for a snack.
You drank a bottle of water.
You ate a baked potato in its skin, with cheese and tomato on top!
You ate a banana for a snack.
You drank a high-sugar soft drink.
You ate a baked potato in its skin.
You made burgers and fries at home.

Index

Glossary

absorbent	Soaks up liquid easily
balsamic vinegar	A vinegar used on foods such as salads and fries
cancer	A disease caused by rapid growth of diseased cells
canola oil	An oil that contains oil from canola seeds
compost bin	A bin where fruit and vegetable scraps rot to form rich, healthy fertiliser for the garden
minerals	Natural substances found in rocks and earth which the human body needs for good health
nutritionist	An expert in healthy foods for the human body
processed foods	Foods that have been made by humans in factories using chemicals
safflower oil	An oil made from safflower seeds
vitamins	Natural substances, mostly found in foods, needed in varying amounts for good health